WHISPER™
THE WINGED UNICORN

Journey to Julie's Heart

Concept by Amber Milligan
Written by Christopher Brown and Jill Wolf
Illustrated by Tom Kinarney
Educational Consultant: JoAnn Mahle, M.A., Ed.

Copyright © 1986 Antioch Publishing Company
ISBN 0-89954-544-0
Made in the United States of America

 Antioch Publishing Company
Yellow Springs, Ohio 45387

1

"Dorian, I don't know what to do," Whisper the Winged Unicorn told her dragon friend as they walked along in Rainbow Forest one autumn afternoon. "I feel so bored and restless!" she said finally, and just then a sudden breeze shook a few leaves off the nearby trees as if to agree with her. "I've never been tired of Rainbow Forest before," she added. Whisper felt ashamed and disloyal now that she had blurted out her true feelings.

But Dorian didn't seem shocked or surprised. He and Whisper had been friends for a long while. "It may be time for you to travel outside Rainbow Forest," Dorian advised her calmly. "Everyone feels the need to travel from time to time," he said. "You needn't feel guilty about leaving us.

The world extends far beyond the borders of Rainbow Forest. No one can blame you for wanting to see more of it. All we ask is that you take care of yourself and come back to us. Ours is a land of magic. It protects us. But whether or not that magic will follow you into distant lands is a question none can answer. You'll be quite on your own."

"But I'll worry about you while I'm gone," Whisper said. "I have a responsibility to my friends."

"That may be so," agreed Dorian, "but you have a responsibility to yourself that's equally important. Besides, the experience you gain may benefit those of us who remain behind. You'll have exciting tales to tell when you return."

"Yes, I suppose I will," murmured Whisper, feeling a tingle of fear, curiosity, and anticipation as she thought about brand-new adventures. "Maybe I'll make even *more* friends," she said, brightening at the prospect. "But first I'll have to say goodbye to old friends. I think, Dorian, I might miss *you* most of all."

"Thank you, Whisper." Dorian nodded and smiled at her. "But you will be able to cope."

"What will I do when I need your wise counsel and advice out in the world?" Whisper asked him.

"Just try to think of what I would do," replied Dorian. "And remember, Whisper, you have special powers within you that you haven't even used or realized yet. Perhaps this journey will help you to grow into those powers. The more you learn about the world and those who live in it, Whisper, the more you learn about yourself, too."

"You make it sound so wonderful and important," said Whisper with a sigh. "Now I feel I really should make this journey. I'll leave tomorrow before I change my mind."

So the very next day, Whisper's friends gathered in the center of Rainbow Forest to wish her a fond farewell.

Whisper had never realized that she had so many friends. It seemed all of Rainbow Forest was there—birds, squirrels, chipmunks, raccoons, and deer. Dorian stood silently to one side while Bixby and Jonathan pressed close to Whisper, their big rabbit eyes blurred with tears. Phineas tried to show Whisper maps and charts from his books. He talked so quickly that the directions he gave Whisper only confused her.

Grandmother Bear had baked some red berry tarts for Whisper to take along on her trip, but Bixby and Jonathan began to gobble them down. They had to keep busy, eating so they wouldn't cry in front of Whisper.

"Stay out of those, you young rascals!" Grandmother Bear warned them. She folded up the napkin and started to give it to Whisper. "Here you are, Whisper—something for the trip," she said. Then she felt the napkin. "Well, for heaven's sakes!" she cried. "There aren't any left to take. Those young rascals ate them all!"

"We're sorry," said Bixby and Jonathan. They looked so sad that they were almost funny and everyone smiled.

"That's alright," Whisper forgave them. "And thank you for the thought, Grandmother Bear. I'll miss you all," Whisper said breathlessly and swallowed hard to keep from crying.

"We'll be thinking of you, Whisper!" cried Jonathan and Bixby.

"Hurry home, child," said Grandmother Bear.

"Have a safe journey," said Phineas.

Dorian looked steadily at Whisper with eyes full of encouragement and love.

"Goodbye, everyone!" called Whisper and launched herself into the air. She circled above her friends once and they waved, then she took off for unknown skies.

Whisper flew on and on through the canyon of clouds. Beneath her the blue sea sparkled, above her the orange sky burned. What lay behind and what lay ahead were blocked from view. The wind which carried her was warm and steady, as soft as her bed in the forest glade. Whisper had learned to sleep while she flew, awakening sometimes in daylight, sometimes in darkness. She had no idea where she was nor how many days had passed since she'd left Rainbow Forest. Two days, maybe even three—it didn't seem to matter. The journey thus far had been like a series of dreams. One of those dreams was the memory of her conversation with her old friend Dorian.

That conversation left a warm spot in Whisper's heart. No matter how far she traveled, the love she shared with her forest friends remained with her. Perhaps that alone was the magic of which Dorian spoke.

Far below, the color of the sea began to change from blue to emerald green. Whisper knew it meant the nearness of land. A thrill of anticipation rippled along her spine. Soon she would be involved in new adventures. She could hardly wait.

School was out in Greenmont. A line of yellow busses waited at the curb while a mob of eager, laughing students jostled aboard. There was one child, however, who wasn't overjoyed. Her name was Julie. She had blue eyes and brown hair, and was about eleven years old. She stood to one side, bewildered, clutching her book bag as though it were a teddy bear. Being small for her age and shy, Julie was the sort of person who was easily overlooked. And that's what seemed to be happening. Julie was a new student, a stranger in a strange place. No one took any notice of her, and she was badly in need of help. Julie didn't know which of these snarling yellow busses she was supposed to get on, and she was beginning to panic.

The whole day had been like that—one long embarrassment. First she'd had mud spattered on her dress. Then she'd wandered into the wrong classroom and had to be led like a lost puppy to the right one. In the lunch line, some kid had finally said, "Hi," but had gone off to sit with someone else. Julie felt lonely and resentful.

The first bus in line drove away. "Probably *mine*," groaned Julie. The farm her dad had recently bought was far out in the country, too far to walk even if she'd known the way.

"Are you lost?" a stern voice demanded.

Startled, Julie looked up to see a tall young teacher glaring at her. "I-I c-can't remember my bus number," she admitted with a blush.

"Name?" the teacher growled. When Julie told him, he consulted a list on his clipboard. "Bus number six. Hurry up or you'll miss it."

Julie thanked him and raced up the steps of bus number six. It was noisy and crowded, not an empty seat anywhere. Julie stood there, more embarrassed than ever. Why was this happening? Didn't *anybody* care? Finally the driver pointed to a couple of girls in the first row. "Scoot over," he said. "Make room." Julie perched on the edge of the seat, and the two girls looked at her as though she had a disease.

A moment later bus number six lurched away from the curb and began twisting its way through the countryside. Looking out the window, Julie watched the village of Greenmont with its steeples and clock tower sink into the valley behind. It was a miserable place, far from her old home and her friends. She missed them terribly. She'd *never* felt so unhappy.

Fumbling in her book bag, Julie took out *The Red Dragon of Elinsore,* one of her favorites. She'd read it many times, but she never tired of the thrilling adventures it contained. There were demons, wizards, valiant knights and fair maidens, and right now they seemed like the *only* friends Julie had. She felt guilty about smuggling the book into school. Dad frowned on her choice of reading matter. "All that make-believe will poison your mind," he often said. "The truth is, there aren't a lot of happy endings." Since the death of Julie's mother, he'd become a sad, bitter man. That's why they'd moved, to get away from unpleasant memories and start a fresh new life far from the city.

Julie turned to the chapter where Lord Garth saves Princess Delia from the wicked magician Gore. "Maybe Dad's right," she thought gloomily. "Maybe there aren't really magic kingdoms or mythical beasts." But to Julie the land of Elinsore was far more appealing than the place she lived in now.

The puffy thick clouds had broken up at last. Whisper could see for miles. Below her the countryside seemed to stretch on and on forever. It was a strange land, divided into neat squares with fences. Whisper knew nothing about farming. Of course, Grandmother Bear kept an herb garden back in Rainbow Forest, and she raised a crop of raspberries every year. Otherwise, trees and flowers grew where they liked. Here it was different. The plants stood like soldiers in ordered rows, and there was no forest to speak of—just a few trees tucked in corners or bending over a stream.

Between the fields ran wide black paths very unlike the narrow forest trails Whisper knew. Now and then strange creatures shot along these paths at terrific speed. They looked like shiny insects swerving madly about with no apparent purpose.

"Perhaps they're friendly," thought Whisper. But she'd been in foreign lands before and knew the value of caution. She descended in slow circles, spying out the ground below.

In the middle of the first path was a thin, broken white line. Whisper landed, straddling it. She sniffed the line, wondering why the path was neatly divided into two halves. She heard a distant whooshing noise and saw the sun flash on one of the strange shiny creatures as it rounded a curve.

"Stop!" cried Whisper. "I want to talk to you!"

The creature screeched, veered toward the side of the path, and let out a loud *honk, honk* that sent Whisper flapping off in fright. She looked just in time to see it put on a burst of speed and disappear into the distance, smoke trailing behind.

"That was pretty rude!" grumbled Whisper. "I'll never learn anything about this strange land if they're going to take *that* attitude."

Soon she came to a village unlike any she'd ever seen before. The buildings were huge with sloping roofs and iron fences around them. One or two even had towers! As she fluttered there, Whisper heard a sound coming from one of them—*bong! bong! bong! bong!* She wondered what it meant.

Several more huge shiny insect-like creatures—these long and yellow—were moving out of the village. Despite her previous encounter, Whisper was filled with curiosity. "If I can figure out what they're up to, maybe everything else will begin to make sense." With a strong thrust of her wings, she set off in pursuit. From time to time one of the creatures turned off on a side path. Soon Whisper was following only one.

Then something astonishing happened. The shiny yellow creature came to a halt, red lights blinking. From the front stepped a tiny figure with long brown hair. Whisper gasped. She didn't know what to make of it. The tiny figure stood a moment beside the path, then turned and walked under some trees. The long yellow creature moved on.

Faced with so exciting a discovery, Whisper forgot caution. She tucked up her legs and plunged toward earth.

It was then that the great silver bird attacked her. It came out of the sky with a scream like a tornado, and

Whisper had no time to defend herself. A tremendous blast of air tossed her like a leaf, and something—she never knew what—crashed into her. Whisper's brain exploded in sparks.

Julie trudged up the lane toward home. It didn't feel like home, but that's what she was supposed to call it. Dad was a veterinarian. For years he'd worked in the city treating dogs and cats and canaries. Then after Mom died he said, "It's time for a change." Now they had a house in the country and a barn full of sick farm animals. Maybe Dad was happier, but Julie wasn't. She missed her old life terribly.

The whine of a jet plane halted her. She looked up. A gleaming Boeing 747 was passing overhead. Julie sighed. If only she could be up there with all those lucky passengers. In just a few hours she'd be back with her old friends, back where she was wanted.

What she saw next made her rub her eyes. Something fell from the plane. It came down like a wounded bird, fluttering and flopping. Julie watched it until it vanished behind the trees on the hillside. "I wonder what that was?" she asked herself. Then with a shrug, she picked up her book bag and marched on.

Aunt Martha was waiting on the porch. "How was your first day at school, dear?" she asked cheerfully. Julie made a face. She couldn't find words to express how awful the day had been. Aunt Martha continued, "Your father's at the Garrett farm with a sick heifer. I'll have your dinner ready in a little while."

Aunt Martha had come to live with them after Mom died. She was kind, but often rather fussy. She cocked an ear at a distant sound, exclaiming, "My, what ails that dog?"

Ralph, the family Irish setter, was barking himself silly on the hill.

"Probably chasing rabbits," suggested Julie.

Up in her room, she changed into jeans and a sweat-shirt. Her room wasn't nearly as nice as the one she'd had before. It was dark and dreary and at night much too quiet. "Country life," she muttered. "It's *boring!*"

Aunt Martha called, "Your dad wants you to feed the animals before he gets back!"

"In a minute!"

Julie emptied her book bag on the bed. Out came *The Red Dragon of Elinsore.* She began to read where she'd left off. Lord Garth, sword in hand, was holding off a pack of hungry tworgs while Princess Delia made her escape. The tworgs were cruel and clever. It took all of Lord Garth's strength to keep them back.

"Julie!" Aunt Martha called again. This time she *meant* it.

Groaning, Julie closed the book. One sure thing— Princess Delia never had to feed livestock! Julie paused on the back porch to slip on her boots. Funny, Ralph was still barking. Ordinarily his rabbit-chasing didn't last long —he wasn't fast enough to catch them.

Julie hurried to the barn. Dad's patients were resting comfortably, a black and white cow, an old Shetland pony, and eight pink piglets snuggled against their mother. Julie spent the next half hour lugging grain, hay, and water to their stalls.

When she came out again, the sun was beginning to set. Ralph's barking had become bloodcurdling howls. That wasn't like him. Julie crossed the barnyard, climbed the fence, and called, "Ralph! Here, boy!"

The howling persisted. "Maybe he's in trouble," Julie thought. "After all, Ralph's a *city* dog." She giggled. "Maybe he's found a nest of hungry tworgs."

Joke or not, she picked up a stick before entering the woods. Shadows grew longer as she climbed the hill. Whippoorwills began to call. A soft wind stirred the tops of the trees. Fear made her throat tighten.

"Woof, woof, woooooo!" went Ralph up ahead. Then Julie heard growls and snarls. That wasn't like him either. Ralph was usually just clumsy and friendly. Those fierce noises make her hair stand on the back of Julie's neck.

"Ralph!" she cried, trembling. "Here, boy!"

Whisper lay in a crumpled heap in the brambles. She was dazed, terrified, and for the first time in her life, in pain. One of her silky wings dangled at her side, broken. She was scratched and bleeding and completely helpless in a foreign land without the magic of Rainbow Forest to protect her. She heard night birds in the moaning wind. What if there were dangerous animals prowling in the darkness?

Suddenly she heard a dreadful howling, a sound that stabbed her like a knife. Wolves!

The howling drew nearer. Whisper tried to move. She felt dizzy and sick at the sound of the horrid beast coming toward her. She shivered and jerked. It was hard to breathe.

Then from deep within came an old call to combat. When cornered, unicorns knew how to fight! Whisper ground her teeth, pushed herself up on her forelegs, and lowered her horn.

"I am Whisper the Winged Unicorn!"she cried. "Beware! Approach at your peril!"

The howling became a gurgling growl. Through the brambles Whisper glimpsed a patch of reddish fur. The beast was closing in!

Then she heard another sound, a voice. "Ralph! What's the matter, boy? Tworgs got you?"

Peering into the bramble thicket was the same young creature Whisper had seen before. She was holding tightly to the red beast, controlling it. Her blue eyes widened, her mouth dropped open, and she became as still as a stone. "I must...I must be...dreaming," Julie gasped.

2

Aunt Martha stood on the back porch. "Julie!" she called. "Your dinner's ready!" To herself she muttered, "That child's never around when you want her." She called again. No answer. "Humph! We'll see if she likes her dinner cold."

At that moment a very breathless Julie was stealing out of the barn with a pony halter and a lead rope. She still couldn't believe what she'd found. A *unicorn*—with *wings!* —huddled in the bushes on the hill. Suddenly nothing seemed real, not the hill, not the farm, not even Aunt Martha's cross voice. The world she knew had changed forever.

"Stay here," she'd told the unicorn. "You're hurt. I'm going to help you." Some thought had twinkled through her mind, some thought that wasn't hers. "I'm in pain, I'm frightened."

Julie dashed across the barnyard, leaped over the fence, and tore off through the woods. She feared she would find the unicorn gone, a trick of her imagination. The fantasy books—Dad would say they'd gone to her head.

Ralph was lying just outside the thicket. He was calm now, whimpering softly as though the unicorn's pain were *his* pain, too.

"There, there," crooned Julie. She eased through the brambles. "Don't be afraid, I won't hurt you."

The same thought came again. "I'm hurt, I'm frightened."

"Yes, I know," said Julie, touching the unicorn's velvety muzzle. "That's why I'm going to take care of you."

"I want to go home," the unicorn told her. The words were like tiny lights in Julie's brain. "I want my friends."

"I'll be your friend," Julie offered. "I'll take you home. I haven't any friends either."

The unicorn sniffed her outstretched hand. "I want to trust you. I'm all alone."

"I'm all alone, *too*," Julie said. "Do you have a name?"

"Whisper—it's the name I was born with."

"That's very beautiful. My name's Julie."

"Also very beautiful," the unicorn said. "Someone must have loved you very much to give you such a name."

"My mother. She died."

Whisper sighed. "That happens," she said. "My friend Dorian says that death is just a change into something better. He's very wise."

Julie shook out the pony halter. "I'm going to slip this over your head. Do you think you can stand?"

Whisper allowed Julie to buckle the leather halter around her neck. Then, wincing, she pushed herself up on all fours. She wobbled, caught herself, and managed to stay up. The useless wing dragged on the ground.

"One step at a time," said Julie, holding the lead rope. "That's it. You don't have far to go."

Slowly, with Ralph scouting ahead, Julie led her new unicorn friend down the hill.

The old brown Chevy van rattled up the lane and stopped by the front porch. Painted on the side was a sign: VALLEY VETERINARY SERVICES. The door opened and Julie's father climbed out. He was tired and muddy and wanted his dinner. In the gleam of the porch light, he knelt to unlace his boots.

"Julie!" he called, entering the house in his stocking feet. "I'm home." He was anxious to hear about her first day of school. Julie was shy and didn't adjust to changes very well. She'd been uprooted, put down again in a strange new environment. Dad knew it must be hard. But life was like that. You had to take the bad with the good.

It was Aunt Martha who came to greet him.

"Where's Julie?" Dad asked.

"I haven't seen her since feeding time. She wasn't very happy when she got home from school. You don't suppose she's run off, do you?"

Dad sighed, picking up his boots again. "I'll go look for her," he said. Then at the back door he paused. "Martha, did you see anything *unusual* today?"

"What do you mean?" Aunt Martha asked.

"Well, somebody stopped by the Garrett farm while I was there. He said he saw some kind of giant white bird sitting in the middle of the highway. Claims his car nearly ran over it. The poor fellow was pale as a ghost. In town, too, they're saying something big and white flew right over the courthouse."

Aunt Martha snorted. "Hogwash!" she declared. "Next it'll be UFO's and little green men."

"I guess you're right," Dad said. "Sounds like one of Julie's stories, doesn't it?" He went out.

Lights glowed in the barn. From the back porch, Dad heard the sound of water running in a bucket and his daughter's voice drifting across the barnyard. At least she hadn't run away.

"Rainbow Forest must be a wonderful place," said Julie. "You'll have to tell me all about it when you're better. Do you really have a friend who's a dragon? Wow!"

Dad shook his head. Things were getting out of hand with that child. It was one thing to have an active imagination, another to live every minute in a world of make-believe. It wasn't healthy. How could he prepare Julie for all the problems life had in store if all she *did* was daydream?

Through a crack in the barn door, he saw the top of Julie's head bobbing in the far stall. Dad knew that stall was empty. She was talking to herself!

"You must be hungry," Julie said. "Do unicorns eat hay?"

"Now that's it!" Dad thought angrily. Then a small voice seemed to twinkle in his brain. "Yes, I'm very fond of hay," it said. Dad frowned, touching his temples.

The barn door squeaked when he opened it. Julie popped out of the stall, running toward him. "Oh, Dad, you aren't going to believe it! We need your help. I told her how good you are with animals."

"What are you talking about?" Dad demanded, but Julie was already dragging him toward the far stall. It wasn't empty after all. Dad stood there and stood there, his eyes taking in the delicate creature lying on the straw. The mystery of the great white "bird" was solved.

Very quietly he said, "I must be losing my presence of mind."

Julie sat cross-legged with Whisper's head on her lap. She watched as her father filled a syringe from a small glass vial. "This won't hurt," Dad said to Whisper. "It'll ease the pain while I work on your wing." Then he laughed. "Imagine a vet explaining medical procedures to his patient. Julie, tell me I'm not crazy."

But it was the unicorn who said, "I'm sure you're quite sane."

Julie laughed too. Down-to-earth Dad had come face to face with a fairy tale! But he was a good vet. Any hurt animal, real *or* imaginary, would receive the best care he could possibly give.

Whisper felt drowsy. The injection had begun to take effect. "Some kind of magic," she thought. "Dorian would be very interested." Soon she began to dream about flowers, millions and millions of flowers singing in the gentle breezes of Rainbow Forest.

Tut Tuttle, the postman, stood on the front porch chatting with Aunt Martha. It was sunny, just the sort of morning to stop and gossip and maybe accept a cup of coffee if it was offered.

"Yes, ma'am," said Mr. Tuttle, "they say that white bird was as big as a horse. Didn't see it myself, mind you, but Mrs. Knox says it threw a shadow across her lawn like a low-flying airplane. Even the *mayor* saw it."

Aunt Martha *cluck, cluck, clucked.* "I don't believe a word of it," she said. "Sunspots or something, that's all."

"I wouldn't be too sure," insisted Tut Tuttle. "When so many people claim to see something, you've *got* to wonder."

"Piffle! Probably just indigestion."

Discouraged, Mr. Tuttle dug in his mail pouch. "Is the doc around?" he asked. "Got a package for him. Medicine, I reckon. Needs signing for."

"He and Julie are down in the barn, been there all night, though I can't imagine why." Aunt Martha *cluck, cluck, clucked* a second time. "Her dad must be getting soft. I'll sign."

"No, no!" Mr. Tuttle whisked the package out of reach. "I'm mighty particular. Got to hand it over to him myself."

"Whatever you like," snapped Aunt Martha. "But you'll get muddy."

Mr. Tuttle slogged across the barnyard and through the half-open door. "Got a package for you, Doc," he called cheerily.

"Wait!" Julie cried, but Tuttle was too fast. Pencil and receipt book in hand, he leaned into the stall.

"Just sign here...uh...uh..."

Tuttle's eyes rolled up and he fainted into the straw at Whisper's feet.

"Oh, dear," said the unicorn, sniffing him.

"What are we going to do now?" wailed Julie.

Dad felt Mr. Tuttle's pulse. "How should I know? Aunt Martha says he's the biggest blabbermouth in the county. The last thing our patient needs is a herd of busybodies nosing around."

Julie glanced at Whisper. The injured wing was splinted and bandaged securely to her body. Her scratches had been washed and salved with ointment, then her coat had been given a good brushing. "When can she fly, Dad?" Julie asked. "You know, just in case she has to get away."

"Good grief, child, I haven't the slightest idea. Until last night I didn't even *believe* in unicorns. My medical knowledge of the species is limited. It might take days, or weeks."

Tut Tuttle groaned and stirred.

"Quick!" said Dad. "We've got to get him out of here." He caught Tuttle under the arms and began to drag him toward the barn door. "Julie, his cap! Bring it."

In the barnyard Mr. Tuttle's heels dug trenches in the mud. They got him to the back porch. Dad called, "Martha, it's Mr. Tuttle. He's passed out."

Aunt Martha came running with a glass of water. Since Mr. Tuttle wasn't in any condition to sip it, she dashed it in his face. He sputtered, opened his eyes, and sat up.

"I saw it! I saw it! The white bird. Only it wasn't a bird. It was a...a..."

"You saw a pony," Dad lied. "That's all, Mr. Tuttle. Just one of my patients, old Roscoe the Shetland pony."

Mr. Tuttle turned frightened eyes toward the barn. "N-no, sir! That wasn't any pony. It was—"

Aunt Martha lashed out with her sharp tongue. "It all comes from too active an imagination, Tut Tuttle. White bird indeed! Hysterics, pure and simple."

Angrily the postman snatched his cap from Julie's trembling hand. "I know what I saw," he insisted with dignity. Tuttle swayed, steadying himself on the porch rail, then marched around the house to his truck. The others followed.

"You've got something spooky in that barn, Doc. I know it!"

With that, Mr. Tuttle bounced off down the lane.

"All right, you two," said Aunt Martha. "What have you got in the barn? No use playing innocent. I know a lie when I hear one."

Julie and Dad exchanged glances. Should they tell or shouldn't they? Finally Dad nodded.

"Can you stand a shock, Aunt Martha?" Julie asked.

"Land sakes! Living with you two, I can stand anything. What's in the barn, child? A dragon?"

"No," answered Julie. "A *unicorn*."

It didn't take long for Tut Tuttle to spread the story around Greenmont. "That new vet's got some kind of monster in his barn. I thought there was something strange about those folks. You should have seen it! Horns and glowing eyes..."

The townspeople were skeptical. They knew very well how Tuttle liked to gossip. But when the rumors reached Sheriff Billings Saturday afternoon, he decided to nip them in the bud. He walked over to Mary's Diner that evening where Tuttle was telling everyone over and over again how the monster not only had horns, but wings, too.

People at the counter and in the booths listened with smiles on their faces as Tuttle rose from his chair and waved his arms to describe the mysterious creature better. They all looked up when Sheriff Billings walked in. He sat at the counter and ordered a cup of coffee. Tuttle sat down, too.

"What's this I hear, Tuttle, about some monster you claim you saw on the new vet's farm?"

"It was the strangest critter I've ever seen," Tuttle said stubbornly. "It had four legs, hooves, and horns— and wings!"

"Guess you don't know enough about farm animals to recognize a cow, a goat, or a pony when you see one." Sheriff Billings chuckled and everyone laughed along with him except Tuttle.

"I know what I saw," insisted Tuttle.

"Just like that UFO you swore you saw last summer when you were fishing at night at Greenmont Lake," said the sheriff and everyone laughed even harder, remembering that the UFO had turned out to be a low-flying airplane.

"You can laugh if you like," said Tuttle, "but what about that giant white bird that flew over the courthouse and landed near the Garrett farm?"

"It was probably just a stray scagull or a runaway goose from someone's farm," said Sheriff Billings. "But if it will make you feel any better, I'll check it out with the vet. I'm sure there's a logical explanation for what you saw today, Tuttle. The rest is just people's imaginations running wild."

Sheriff Billings finished his coffee and walked out of the diner. Ripples of laughter and a new wave of conversation followed in his wake. In the privacy of his office, he dialed the vet's number.

Julie's father was in the kitchen with Aunt Martha and Julie when the phone rang. They were eating dinner and he impatiently scraped back his chair to go answer it.

"I hope it's not another animal to tend to at suppertime," muttered Aunt Martha, stabbing at her food with her fork. "A body can't sit through a decent meal without some sick cow trying to butt in."

But Julie wasn't listening to her Aunt Martha's complaints. She was trying to hear what Dad was saying. Julie had worried all day about what Tut Tuttle would tell everyone in town. She was afraid this phone call was about Whisper.

"Yes, Sheriff Billings, Mr. Tuttle did seem rather upset when he left our place today," Julie's dad was saying. "I guess the sight of a sick animal is an upsetting thing to some people." He paused. "No, no. I would certainly never perform any dangerous or illegal experiments on any of my patients. Well, yes, I understand. I'm glad you feel that way. Thank you for calling."

As he hung up the phone, Julie rushed over to him. "Dad, what was that about? Was it about Whisper?"

"Yes." He sighed. "That was Sheriff Billings and I had to do some careful talking. Mr. Tuttle has spread the word around town that we have some strange monster hidden in our barn."

"I wish I could lay my hands on that silly man. He'd be seeing stars, not just unicorns, when I finished with him," declared Aunt Martha with a frown, but Julie knew Aunt Martha would never hurt a soul.

"At least Sheriff Billings believes Tuttle was seeing things," said Julie's dad. "Thank goodness for small favors. It gives us some time to help Whisper heal before anything else happens to her."

Julie hugged her father. "Oh, Dad, I know you'll make Whisper as good as new! And we won't let anything happen to her either."

"Now don't get too attached to her, Julie," warned her dad. "We don't know what will happen. We're dealing with the unknown."

Julie wasn't listening. She was already making plans to keep Whisper. Whisper would be the most fantastic pet any girl ever had!

After supper Julie rushed out to the barn to talk to her new friend.

"Whisper, you're safe—for now anyway!" Julie told her as she gently petted her. "Nobody believes that tattletale Mr. Tuttle. You can stay here with us until your wing heals. You can stay here with me forever!"

Whisper nodded sleepily. She was too tired to disagree with anything Julie said. It felt good to find friends after the painful and bewildering experiences of the car, plane, and other strange machines. Dorian had been right about the world—she was learning about all kinds of things, both bad and good.

"Go to sleep now, Whisper. Dad says you need lots of rest," said Julie and carefully draped a blanket over Whisper. "Goodnight! Sweet dreams!" she called as she shut the door to the barn.

3

On Sunday Julie spent most of the afternoon with Whisper, keeping her company, along with Ralph and the sick animals in the barn. She had her copy of *The Red Dragon of Elinsore* with her, and while she nestled cozily between Whisper and a bale of hay, she read the story out loud.

"So what do you think? Isn't it a great story?" Julie asked Whisper.

"Yes, it is. I'm glad there aren't any tworgs in Rainbow Forest!" Whisper flashed her heartfelt opinion back to Julie.

"Where is Rainbow Forest? Is it like Elinsore?" Julie asked eagerly.

"I'm not quite sure where Rainbow Forest is from here," Whisper told her doubtfully. "I'd have to be up in the clouds to get my bearings again. I hope that airplane didn't knock out my sense of direction, too. Rainbow Forest isn't exactly like Elinsore. There aren't any people that I know of—except for Phineas, but he's really a Nodkin."

"Nodkins sound nice," interrupted Julie. "Do you have lots of friends in Rainbow Forest?"

"Yes," said Whisper. "I miss them very much. There's Bixby and Jonathan and…" She started to tremble, feeling a little homesick.

"It's alright." Julie gave her a sympathetic pat on the shoulder. "Let's talk about something else."

"You're very kind." Whisper blinked back her tears and smiled. "So is your father."

"I guess he is," Julie said slowly. "He's very good with animals. But sometimes I've wondered if he really loves me. He always seems to be mad or tired. Ever since my mother died, it hasn't been the same for us. I really miss her. Sometimes it hurts a lot."

"Maybe your father feels hurt inside, too," suggested Whisper. "He must have loved your mother very much and I'm sure he loves you as much. Maybe he doesn't mean to be mean—he just seems that way because he feels so sad."

"I never thought about the way *he* felt before. I suppose you're right, Whisper," said Julie. "You're just as wise as your friend Dorian the dragon."

"Really?" Whisper turned pink, feeling very pleased. "Maybe I'm growing up just as Dorian said I would."

"Sometimes it seems like I'll never grow up," said Julie.

"Why do you want to grow up?" asked Whisper.

"Then I could do what I wanted. I could have a horse of my own, and never go to school, and have great adventures like Lord Garth and Lady Delia." Julie picked up the book again. "Would you like to hear more about them?"

"Oh, yes," said Whisper.

Julie continued reading. The sound of her soft, high voice made Whisper drowsy and soon she was asleep. Julie wasn't far behind, slumping against Whisper's warm shoulder, with the book still in her lap. Aunt Martha found them that way when she went to call Julie in for supper. "Poor, sweet lambs," she murmured as she bent over and touched Julie's arm to awaken her.

The next morning Julie wandered into the barn very early. She looked miserable.

"What's wrong?" asked Whisper.

"Dad's making me go to school. I want to stay here with you. It's not fair. I hate school."

"What's school?" asked Whisper. Julie explained that it was a place of learning. "But why do you hate learning?"

"I don't hate learning. It's my new school. Nobody will even talk to me."

"Maybe it's because they're afraid of you. We always fear what we don't understand. When I first saw you, I was terrified. I didn't know anything about you. Soon I discovered what a gentle, loving creature you are. Others will notice, too, as soon as you show them. In Rainbow Forest we live together in harmony. We understand each other and appreciate our differences. My best friend is a dragon as big as an oak tree. You wouldn't think we'd have much in common, but we do. Both of us must try to understand the world. Then we'll never be afraid. When fear leaves, love comes. That's the magic of Rainbow Forest. I thought I'd left it behind me, but I found it here in *you*."

"But nobody's interested in me," Julie insisted. "Nobody smiles or talks."

"You smile first," said Whisper. "You talk first. You have to give others a chance. Otherwise you'll turn out like Mr. Tuttle, suspicious of everything, afraid of the monster in the barn. You and I know there never was a monster. Maybe someday he will, too."

Julie got up, brushing the straw from her school clothes. "All right," she agreed. "I'll walk in there with a smile on my face and say 'hi' to everybody."

"Good for you," said Whisper.

Julie walked down the lane to catch the bus. In spite of Whisper's words of encouragement, she still felt shy. She was overwhelmed by the prospect of new faces and strange places. Julie was afraid, too, that she might have tons of schoolwork to catch up on if she was behind her class at this school.

When the bus approached, lights flashing, all the old feelings of dread welled up inside her. Her feet felt heavy and the bus steps seemed too high to climb. On the top step Julie tripped and fell forward, flat on her stomach.

The contents of her book bag flew down the aisle. Kids laughed, and even applauded. "Oh, no," Julie thought, getting up slowly, totally humiliated.

"Quiet!" the bus driver shouted, then leaned toward Julie. "Are you okay?"

"Y-yes," replied Julie, somewhat shaken. She looked around for her books. A girl who looked to be Julie's own age handed them to her and sat down again.

The bus driver was waiting for Julie to find a seat. Julie remembered Whisper's words about being friendly first. She sat down next to the girl who had picked up her books for her.

Julie gave her a smile. "Hi! My name's Julie. Thanks for picking up my books."

To Julie's surprise, the girl turned and smiled at her, seeming just as surprised that Julie had spoken to her. "Hi. I'm Kim. I live on the farm next to yours. I'm in your class at school, too."

"I'm sorry—I guess I don't remember you. I was too scared the other day to really look at anybody," said Julie.

"You'll get to know all of us soon enough," Kim told her. "It's not a very big school. Are you reading that book for a book report or something?" Kim pointed to *The Red Dragon of Elinsore*.

"No. But it's my favorite book."

"Mine, too."

"You've read it?" cried Julie.

"Yes. The part I like best is when Lord Garth saves Lady Delia from the tworgs by using his magic ring."

"Mine, too," said Julie. She felt a warm glow inside from discovering that she shared something special with someone she'd thought was a stranger. It made them seem like friends already.

"Did you know there's another book that follows it?" asked Kim. "It's called *Revenge of the Tworgs*. My mom bought it for me for my birthday. I'll lend it to you when I'm done with it."

"There's a second book of Elinsore adventures?" Julie couldn't believe her good luck. More of Lady Delia and Lord Garth—and a good friend to share their adventures with, too. "I can't wait to read it," Julie told Kim.

All the way to school, they talked about *The Red Dragon of Elinsore* and other books they'd read. When the teacher realized that they had become friends, she asked Kim to help Julie and show her the way around school. They ate lunch at the same table in the cafeteria.

Julie noticed that Kim didn't seem to have many friends either. "It's hard to have friends when you live so far from town," explained Kim. "That's the one bad thing about living on the farm. No one wants to come out to see you. But I like it anyway. Mom says maybe next summer I can get a horse."

"Then my dad could take care of it. He's a vet," said Julie. "He's really good with animals."

"Does your mom like animals, too?"

Julie lowered her eyes. "She died."

"Oh, I'm sorry. But I thought I saw...I mean..." Kim stammered, unsure what to say.

"You mean you saw Aunt Martha," spoke up Julie. "After my mom died, Aunt Martha came to live with us. Then we moved out here from the city."

"What is it like in the city?" asked Kim. "Is it like it is on TV?"

Julie smiled. "Not exactly like TV. But there are lots of things to do. I guess I miss it."

The bell rang then and lunch was over. All through afternoon classes, Julie felt happier, thinking about her new friend and about going home soon to see Whisper. Whisper had been right about making friends. Julie had made the first move and now she felt as if she'd known Kim for a long time. Julie couldn't wait to get home to tell Whisper all about her day at school.

When Julie got off the bus and started up the lane, Ralph ran to meet her. He jumped up and down, wagging his tail and barking. They raced up the lane together.

Julie rushed into the house, threw down her book bag, and immediately grabbed the feed buckets off the back porch.

"Well! Someone's in a big hurry," commented Aunt Martha. "Never seen a child in such a hurry to feed livestock and do chores."

"Hi, Aunt Martha. Did you feed Whisper today?"

"Yes, and I fed Ralph, too. Can't neglect that dog just because of a new pet."

"But Whisper is different. She's hurt. She's probably lonely in that old barn."

"She's got Roscoe and all the others to talk to," said Aunt Martha. "Don't worry. I looked after Whisper. And we had a nice little talk, too. Heaven knows, if you'd told me one day I'd be spending my morning talking to a unicorn, I'd have said 'Hogwash!'"

Aunt Martha had such a funny expression on her face, Julie grinned.

"Maybe I should feed Whisper again," she said and opened the door.

"Now, wait just a minute." Aunt Martha pretended to frown. "This unicorn business isn't going to keep you from your homework, I hope."

"I'll do it later," Julie called and let the door slam. Aunt Martha shook her head as she watched Julie run to the barn.

"Oh, Whisper, you were right!" Julie greeted her. "I smiled first and made a friend. Her name's Kim and she lives on the next farm, she's in my class, and she even likes *The Red Dragon of Elinsore!*"

"That's wonderful!" Whisper tried to get to her feet, but Julie stopped her.

"No, not yet, Whisper. Dad says you should lie still until he's sure your wing is set. Would you like some oats? I hope these are okay. I don't think I could eat oats, but I guess they're alright for you. I mean, I don't really know what unicorns eat."

Julie went on and on, and Whisper let her, for she knew Julie was talking more because she was happier now, and that made Whisper feel happy, too. She smiled as Julie groomed her, running the brush carefully around her sore spots.

Next Julie put down fresh straw in Whisper's stall and when she was finally satisfied that Whisper was comfortable, she fed the other animals.

"I'll have Dad check you later, Whisper," Julie promised and went back to the house.

"You seem awfully happy," said Aunt Martha when Julie returned to the house. "Did you have a good day at school?"

"It was a lot better today," said Julie. "I did what Whisper said and I already have a new friend." As Julie helped Aunt Martha make supper, she told her about Kim.

"I'm glad you made a friend," Aunt Martha said. "Maybe now you won't be moping around the house with your nose stuck in a book all day."

"Oh, Kim likes *The Red Dragon of Elinsore,* too!" Julie told her. "She's even going to lend me the second book in the series!"

Aunt Martha sighed, but she was smiling to herself. They heard the van coming up the lane then and Julie quickly set the table.

Before Dad even got his boots off, Julie was out on the porch. "Dad, will you check Whisper?"

"After supper," he said wearily. "I'm a little tired right now. I spent most of the day answering questions and trying to brush off bad jokes about what Tut Tuttle saw."

"You don't think anyone will come out here looking for Whisper?" Julie looked worried.

"No. People seem to think it's more of a joke. I think we're safe for now." He held the door open and they went inside the house.

After supper Julie followed her father out to the barn. "Hello, Whisper," said Julie's dad and Whisper greeted him cheerfully. He carefully examined her wing and the cuts. "Well, I think everything looks alright," he told Julie. "Her cuts are healing and her wing is set properly and starting to mend. We'll just have to wait and see."

"When will she be up and around?" Julie asked anxiously.

"Maybe tomorrow we'll get her on her feet. I want to be sure she's alright before she starts walking around. On the other hand, I don't want her to get stiff lying down for too long. It might feel different for her, standing and walking with her wing taped to her side."

Julie listened to her father, thinking how good he was with animals and realizing it was because he was wise and kind.

Whisper read her mind. "I told you he was," she said to Julie and Julie's dad picked up the thought.

"What did you tell me?" he asked, giving Whisper and Julie puzzled looks.

"Nothing, Dad," Julie spoke up quickly. "Whisper's thinking about something we talked about yesterday." Julie gave him a hug and he seemed surprised but pleased.

He made Whisper comfortable for the night, checked his other patients, then turned to Julie before he left. "Don't stay out here too long," he told her. "Remember you've got homework."

Julie settled down beside Whisper, petting her and playing with her mane. She twined it into little braids, then brushed them out with her fingers. "I hope you weren't too lonely today, Whisper, while I was gone."

"I missed you," replied Whisper. "But Ralph and Roscoe kept me company—and the piglets are very talkative, too."

"Well, I wish I could be with you all day. Wait until next summer. We'll go exploring together all over the farm. We'll have lots of good times." Julie hugged Whisper.

Whisper closed her eyes and tried not to communicate what she was thinking to Julie. She loved Julie but she was also homesick for Rainbow Forest. Whisper wanted to stay with Julie, but she wanted to go home someday, too. She wasn't sure whether she could live in this strange world of machines and people, and she missed all of her old friends in Rainbow Forest. When she was well, Whisper knew she would probably have to go.

In the house, Julie's dad and Aunt Martha were thinking about the same thing.

"I think this unicorn is a real mixed blessing, Bill," Aunt Martha was saying. "It's really perked Julie up, but she's getting so attached to Whisper that it'll break her heart if Whisper's taken away. That unicorn has made her forget some of the hurt of her mom's passing away, but it's all going to come back if that unicorn goes."

"I know, Martha. I don't know about this unicorn business either. I'd like to keep Whisper until we're sure she's fit. But we can't keep her forever because we can't keep her hidden away forever. Someone's bound to find out sooner or later." Julie's dad sighed. "Then think of the publicity," he said. "Newspapers, television, photographers tramping all over the place. Whisper could never be Julie's pet. She'd be a sideshow item. And think of the animal, too. Wherever Whisper came from, she certainly would be happier back there. Maybe Julie's tougher than you think. She'll realize what's best for Whisper and she knows that life has its losses." He sighed again and rubbed his forehead. "Although it seems she's already had more than her share."

"I just don't know," said Aunt Martha. "I'd hate to see her hurt and her heart broken. I don't want to be the one to tell her that she can't keep Whisper forever. If there was any way we could keep that unicorn and spare her that hurt, I'd try it."

"You're a good person, Martha," said Julie's dad and patted her hand. "Guess I'd better go get Julie out of that barn, or she'll be there all night," he added, smiling.

4

The following morning Julie sat down next to Kim on the bus. She started to talk about all the fun things the two of them could do next summer when school was out. Then she noticed that Kim seemed different today—she wasn't smiling.

"What's wrong?" asked Julie.

"I talked to my mom and dad last night about getting a horse so we could take turns riding next summer. But they don't think they'll be able to afford it."

"Don't worry. I've got something better than a horse," bragged Julie without thinking.

"What do you mean?"

"It's a secret, but I'll tell you someday," replied Julie hastily, realizing she'd said the wrong thing.

Kim looked at her suspiciously. "When I told my mom and dad about you last night, they said the people in town have been talking about you and your dad because you have some kind of weird animal on your place."

"That's just a story Tattletale Tuttle made up," responded Julie. "My Aunt Martha says he just likes to gossip."

"He's a nerd," said Kim with a giggle. "One day last summer, he brought a letter for mom to sign for, and he was wearing Bermuda shorts. His knees looked like doorknobs!"

The girls giggled together, friends again. Julie was glad that Kim didn't talk anymore about the animal *rumors*. Some of the other kids at school did give Julie strange looks, but she didn't let it bother her. She was getting used to her new school and some kids thought it was neat that her dad was a vet. Besides, the thought of Whisper helped Julie through the rough moments—like her arithmetic class, when she couldn't figure out how to do the problems on the board.

By the end of the week, Julie felt as if she'd attended Greenmont School for a long time. She and Kim were becoming good friends. Every afternoon when they boarded the bus to go home, they headed for the very back seat. Whenever the bus went over the dips in the rough country roads, the back seat bounced up and down, and so did Kim and Julie. They laughed as they bumped against each other.

One evening Kim's mother called Aunt Martha to ask if Julie would like to go home with Kim after school the next day, then stay for supper. Kim's dad would drive her home later.

"I think you should go. It was nice of them to invite you," Aunt Martha told Julie.

"But what about Whisper?" wailed Julie. "I always visit her after school. She'll miss me."

"She'll understand. I'll take care of her. Don't worry," said Aunt Martha.

"Okay, I'll go." Julie sighed.

"Kim is your friend, too, you know. And I think you should invite her to come here sometime," added Aunt Martha.

"I can't!" Julie protested. "She might find out about Whisper. Then something will happen to Whisper."

"If Kim is your friend, she wouldn't tell your secret."

"Well, I don't know," said Julie.

"You're being selfish about that animal," Aunt Martha told her. "You can't keep her to yourself forever."

"Yes, I can," said Julie in a stubbornly cheerful voice, grabbed Whisper's feed bucket, and headed for the barn. Aunt Martha shook her head.

When Julie went into the barn, Whisper was standing up in her stall.

"Whisper, you're standing up!" cried Julie, putting down the feed bucket.

"Yes, I'm feeling much better," Whisper told her. "I want to walk around a little."

"But you should be careful," Julie said. "Dad says not to try too much at a time."

Julie fed and groomed Whisper, then slowly walked her around the barn, letting her stretch her legs and get back her sense of balance.

"I wish I could take you outside for some fresh air," said Julie, "but someone might see you. I know it must be hard for you, stuck in this old barn all day."

"It's not that awful, but I do miss flying in the open sky," Whisper admitted.

"It must be wonderful to fly. Tell me what it's like," begged Julie.

"I can't describe it to you exactly," said Whisper. "It seems perfectly natural to me because I've done it so much. When I fly, I feel like a feather floating through the air or a fish swimming through cool, clear water. Does that give you any idea of what it's like?"

"Sort of. Isn't it scary, too?"

"Oh, I've had my share of close calls and scares. But colliding with that airplane was the worst experience! I hope I never run into one of those again."

"But I'm glad you landed here so we could help you," said Julie and led Whisper back to her stall.

"I'm glad you were here, too. I was so frightened. I even thought Ralph was a wolf at first."

Julie laughed at the thought of friendly old Ralph as a wolf. "Well, he does howl really loud," she said, "and he might bite someone if they tried to hurt me—or you."

As Whisper settled herself in her stall, Julie sat down on the bale of hay.

"Whisper, I won't be able to see you tomorrow after school," Julie told her. "I'm going to Kim's house. But I'll be back later on."

"I would like to meet Kim," said Whisper.

"But I don't want anyone to know about you, Whisper. They might tell. Then someone would come to take you away."

"Don't you trust Kim?" asked Whisper. "Isn't she your friend?"

Julie hesitated. "Well, yes, I guess she is. But I don't know if I can trust anyone, Whisper. As soon as I trust someone, they hurt me or tell on me or move away—or something," she finished lamely. "But I trust you, Whisper. You're not like people. So I don't want anyone else to know about you. It's bad enough that Dad and Aunt Martha know—they might change their minds and decide to do something about you."

"You should trust your friends, and your aunt and your father," said Whisper. "I'm sure they love you. Sometimes they may do things that seem unfair to you, but they might have reasons that you don't understand yet. Then later you find out that they were right and that they were helping you all the time. At least that's how my friend Dorian explains things."

"But I trusted Mom and she left me!" Julie blurted out suddenly, tears welling up out of nowhere.

"You sound as if you're angry with her," said Whisper. "She couldn't help what happened."

"I'm not really mad," said Julie, quickly wiping her eyes. "But I feel like I must have done something really awful to deserve her dying."

"No, you didn't," said Whisper. "It wasn't because of you. It just happened."

"I know." Julie tried to smile. "Aunt Martha told me that, too. I guess I'm just feeling sorry for myself." She hugged Whisper. "I didn't mean to make you sad, too." Julie picked up *The Red Dragon of Elinsore*. "Since I won't be able to read to you tomorrow, let's finish this tonight," said Julie and began to read.

The next afternoon Julie and Kim both got off the bus at the end of Kim's lane. As they walked up the gravel driveway, Julie saw a white two-story frame house in the distance.

"Your house looks a lot like mine," Julie told Kim. "Do you have a dog?" she asked, thinking of how Ralph rushed out to meet her every afternoon.

"No. We have cats," said Kim. "You can help me feed them later and I'll show you the kittens."

When they reached the house, they went in the back door and entered the kitchen, where a dark-haired woman smiled at Julie.

"Hello. I'm Kim's mother and you must be Julie. I'm glad to meet you. It's nice for Kim to have a friend close by."

"Thank you," Julie said, feeling suddenly shy in the face of a warm welcome.

"Go on—help yourselves," said Kim's mother and Julie saw that she had made chocolate chip cookies and filled two glasses with milk. "But don't spoil your appetites for supper," Kim's mother added with a smile.

She left the girls alone then and went on the back porch where she put on boots and a jacket, and picked up a bucket.

"What is she doing?" Julie asked Kim as they munched their cookies.

"The chores—feeding the chickens and the sheep. Usually I help her, but she said it was okay if I skipped them today—except for feeding the cats."

Julie looked around the big kitchen. "Your house is nice. Aunt Martha says our kitchen is too small. What are we having for dinner?"

"Mom was going to have pot roast but I talked her into hamburgers," said Kim. "I couldn't get her to have pizza. She just doesn't understand what's *really* good," Kim added with a grin.

They laughed and finished their cookies, washing them down with big gulps of milk.

"Now you can help me feed the cats," said Kim, pushing back her chair and carrying their glasses to the sink.

Julie followed her to the back porch where Kim opened a huge refrigerator. She took out a carton of eggs and a gallon of milk. Kim handed Julie a loaf of bread. "Here. Break up all the slices into little pieces and put them in that pan." She pointed to a metal trash can lid on the floor. The lid was turned upside down so that it made a large shallow bowl.

While Julie broke up the bread, Kim cracked eggs into the pan and poured milk over the mixture.

"Yuck! Raw eggs!" Julie pretended to gag. "Are you sure cats like this stuff?"

"They lap up every drop," declared Kim.

"But those eggs are brown!" cried Julie, looking in surprise at the dark eggshells Kim tossed aside.

"Sure. Our chickens laid these. Haven't you ever seen eggs fresh from the farm?" asked Kim.

"No. Just the white kind they sell in the store," said Julie.

"Well, these taste better. And the cats like them, too. Here, carry this." Kim handed Julie another metal trash can lid, as big as the first one, but empty.

"What's this for?"

"You'll see," said Julie.

The girls put on their jackets then carried everything outside. Kim led the way to the side of the barn. She put down the lid full of food, then she took the empty trash can lid from Julie and banged it against the wooden side of the barn. "Here, kitty, kitty, kitty!" shouted Kim.

Julie looked around. There were no cats in sight. Then suddenly, they seemed to come from everywhere, gliding across the yard, under fences, and around buildings. There were at least a dozen of them. They headed for the trash can lid and immediately started to eat.

A few cats were so eager that they stepped in the lid, getting milk on their paws. Kim gently picked them up by the scruff of their necks and put them down outside the pan. All Julie could hear was the sound of cat tongues lapping milk, eggs, and soggy bread.

"Wow, these cats are beautiful!" said Julie. "And there are so many of them."

"You can have one of the kittens," offered Kim.

"Could I? I'd have to ask Dad first. And Ralph!" she added with a laugh, wondering how Ralph would feel about a cat.

"Tell your Aunt Martha that having a cat keeps away the mice," Kim said. "C'mon, I'll show you where the kittens are."

Kim led Julie into the barn where the kittens were hidden in the hayloft. Julie hung back as Kim climbed the ladder.

"What's the matter?" Kim called down.

"I'm afraid to climb that high," said Julie.

"It's okay. I'll hold the ladder for you. And don't look down." Kim leaned over to steady the ladder while Julie climbed up.

The kittens were at the back of the loft, snuggled down in the hay.

"Why does the mother cat keep them up here in the loft?" asked Julie.

"She hides them from the tomcat," explained Kim as they each cuddled a kitten against their chest. "Tomcats can be mean. They'll hurt the kittens."

"I guess I don't know much about farms or farm animals yet," said Julie.

"It's fun showing someone the things I see every day."

"Do you like living on the farm?" asked Julie.

"Sometimes. Then sometimes I wish I lived in town with the other kids. But now that you're here, it won't be so bad."

"Look at this one. It's so cute!" Julie held up a kitten with a gray and white face and a very pink nose. "I think I'd like this one."

"You can have it if your dad says it's okay." Kim put the kittens back in their nest and covered them up. "Let's go back to the house and I'll show you my room."

The girls climbed down the ladder, picked up the empty trash can lids, and went inside the house.

After supper Kim's dad took Julie home in his pickup truck. Kim went along for the ride, squeezing onto the front seat with Julie. As they bumped up and down the farm lanes, it reminded them of their afternoon bus rides.

Kim's father was tall and quiet; he had a beard and wore a baseball cap with a label on it advertising livestock feed.

"I heard rumors in town about your dad having some strange animal on your place, Julie," he said. "But I don't believe all that foolishness. People think they see things and when they tell everyone else about it, it gets blown out of proportion."

"Yes, I guess so," replied Julie, not sure what to say.

"Why, Tut Tuttle swore he saw a UFO last summer at the lake. Wasn't anything but a helicopter or an airplane with its lights on."

He pulled the truck around to Julie's house and she hopped out.

"Thank you," Julie said politely and Kim's dad nodded. "I had a great time," she told Kim. "See you tomorrow at school."

Kim waved to Julie as the truck pulled away. Julie waited for a minute, then instead of going inside the house she ran straight to the barn.

"Whisper, are you awake?" Julie called softly.

"Yes," answered Whisper. "Did you have a good time?"

"We had lots of fun. You should see Kim's room—she has all these posters on the walls with pictures of castles and dragons and horses and unicorns."

"It sounds very nice."

"I hope you weren't too lonely," Julie said guiltily.

"I missed you, but your aunt and your father took care of me. I even walked around the barn by myself. Your father says I'm getting stronger."

"I hope you'll still be able to fly," said Julie.

"I hope so, too," Whisper agreed heartily.

"Maybe we can finish our story now." Julie pulled *The Red Dragon of Elinsore* from her book bag. "If you promise not to fall asleep like you did last night," she teased Whisper.

"I thought I saw a truck come up the lane, then heard voices out here," Aunt Martha said, appearing in the doorway. "It's time for you to come in the house."

Julie looked up. "Oh, Aunt Martha, can't I read to Whisper for a little while?"

"It's getting late. Don't you have homework to do?"

"I did my homework at Kim's. Besides, I keep promising Whisper we'll finish this book. Can't I please stay out here?" Julie begged.

"Well, alright—but not too long."

When Aunt Martha had gone, Julie settled down in the straw and read *The Red Dragon of Elinsore*—and Whisper stayed wide awake to the very end.

5

The next morning when Julie got on the bus, Kim looked upset. "I was going to lend you my copy of the second book of Elinsore," Kim told her, "and I forgot to give it to you last night before you left. Then I forgot to bring it along this morning, too."

"That's okay," said Julie. "You can bring it some other time. Everybody forgets things."

And Julie had forgotten about the book by the time school was over that day. She was in a hurry to get home and spend the whole weekend with Whisper. Julie flew up the lane before Ralph was even halfway down to meet her.

"My, you're always in a hurry these days," commented Aunt Martha. She looked up from the carrots she was slicing for dinner as Julie raced in the house and grabbed Whisper's feed bucket.

"I've got the whole weekend to spend with Whisper," said Julie.

"Now remember you promised to help me bake pies tomorrow," Aunt Martha called after her, but the door had already slammed.

"Hello, Whisper," shouted Julie as she opened the barn door.

"Hello, Julie," came the answer from the direction of Whisper's stall.

Julie fed the other animals, then scooped out some oats for Whisper. She sat down to watch Whisper eat. "Maybe you'd like something different to eat," Julie told Whisper. "What about some carrots or an apple? I'll be right back."

Julie jumped up and ran back to the house, leaving the barn door open. She hadn't noticed a small figure walking across the hill.

"Can I have some carrots and an apple for Whisper?" Julie asked Aunt Martha.

"Well, you can't have these carrots. I just chopped them up for the stew. Let me get some out of the refrigerator." Aunt Martha hurried over to the refrigerator, took out a dozen more carrots, and found a big red apple. "Better wash them first," she said.

Julie cleaned them carefully under the faucet, then wrapped them in a paper towel.

"Next thing you know, you'll be wanting Whisper to have dessert and eat at the table with us," joked Aunt Martha and gave a little snort of laughter.

But Julie barely heard her. She headed for the barn again, her jacket flapping in the wind.

When she arrived at the doorway, Julie thought she heard a sound. She crept quietly into the barn. Someone was standing in front of Whisper's stall, holding a book. It was Kim!

A wave of relief and anger swept over Julie. "Kim!" she exclaimed. "What are you doing here?"

"I brought over *Revenge of the Tworgs*," explained Kim. She handed the Elinsore book to Julie. "Is this the secret you were talking about?" She was speaking to Julie, but she was staring at Whisper. "It's a real unicorn! It's beautiful!" Kim said breathlessly.

"Her name is Whisper," said Julie. "Ralph and I found her lying hurt in the woods after she ran into an airplane."

"So Mr. Tuttle was right. You *do* have a fantastic creature hidden in your barn."

"But you can't tell anyone!" cried Julie. "They'll hurt her or take her away, I know it."

"I promise I won't tell anyone," said Kim. "Can I pet her?"

"Yes. She's very gentle."

Kim reached out slowly and carefully patted Whisper's neck. "Hello, Whisper."

"Hello, Kim!" said Whisper and Kim immediately picked up her silent greeting. She was startled at first and turned to Julie.

"She communicates with us by thought waves," said Julie.

"But where did she come from?" asked Kim.

"From Rainbow Forest. That's where she lives."

"Will her wing be alright?"

"Dad thinks so. We'll have to wait and see," replied Julie.

"Are you going to keep her?"

"I hope so. But we'll have to keep her hidden."

"If people knew you had a real unicorn here…" Kim's voice trailed off.

"It'll be our secret, okay?" Julie looked closely at her friend.

"I promise," said Kim.

"I brought her some carrots and an apple," Julie said.

"Can I help feed her?" Kim asked eagerly.

"Sure."

The two girls offered Whisper the carrots and apple, holding them carefully so their fingers didn't get in the way of Whisper's teeth.

"Ooooo, she tickles!" Kim giggled, almost dropping the apple in the straw as Whisper nuzzled the fruit. "I'm sure I couldn't eat all this stuff. Oats and carrots—yuck!"

"They're delicious," Whisper told her, and Julie and Kim both laughed.

"Julie, you're so lucky," said Kim, running her fingers through Whisper's mane and patting her neck again.

"Whisper even likes *The Red Dragon of Elinsore*," Julie said. "I've been reading it to her every night."

"I bet she comes from a place just like Elinsore."

"Almost," Whisper joined in. "I do have a dragon friend named Dorian."

"This is better than a fairy tale," said Kim.

After Whisper's food had settled, Julie led Whisper around the barn for her walk while Kim watched. As she put Whisper back in her stall, they heard Aunt Martha calling from the house.

"I guess I'd better go now," said Kim. "Can I come over tomorrow and see you and Whisper?"

"Yes. Thanks for bringing the book," said Julie. "And remember—don't tell anyone about you-know-what."

"Goodbye, Kim," Whisper called.

"Goodbye, Whisper." Kim went out the door, still in a daze.

Julie sat down on the bale of hay. "I don't know, Whisper. Kim found you by accident and I don't think I like sharing you with someone else. You were my special secret. Just the same, it's fun having someone else know about you."

"Julie, what's going on?" Aunt Martha entered the barn and looked around. "I thought I saw Kim coming out of here looking as if she'd seen a ghost."

"She was bringing me the book she'd promised to lend and found Whisper."

"Well, she wouldn't do anything to bring harm to Whisper," said Aunt Martha. "Come in now and help me with supper."

When Julie told her father that Kim had discovered Whisper, he seemed concerned. "Well, that does it. Now everyone will know."

"Dad!" groaned Julie. "She promised she wouldn't tell."

"Well, you know how kids are," he muttered.

"Now, some young people keep secrets better than some grown-up blabbermouths I know," Aunt Martha said tartly.

"I suppose you're right." Julie's dad shrugged his shoulders. "We won't worry about that right now. It's too late anyhow. The horse is out of the barn, or should I say, the unicorn."

The next morning Kim showed up while Julie was grooming Whisper.

"It's a beautiful day," Kim greeted them.

"Yes. I wish I could take Whisper outside," said Julie.

"Why don't you? There's nobody around for miles," said Kim. "No one will see us."

"What do you think, Whisper?" Julie asked her.

"It would be lovely to see the sky again," answered Whisper. "I feel fine today."

"Alright." Julie led Whisper to the door while Kim held it open.

Whisper emerged from the barn into the autumn sunshine, blinking her eyes in the bright light.

"This is our place, Whisper," Julie told her.

Whisper gazed about, taking in the old farmhouse, the woods, the lane, the hill, the pond, the green grass and golden leaves, and the blue sky.

"Why, this place is not much unlike Rainbow Forest," said Whisper in surprise.

She walked back and forth, exploring the area between the house and barn. Julie and Kim let her stroll around for a while, then led her safely back inside the barn.

They hadn't noticed a small truck parked by the mailbox at the end of the lane. Inside the truck sat Mr. Tuttle, holding a pair of binoculars to his eyes, the same binoculars he had carried in his truck all week, hoping for a glimpse of what he'd just seen.

"Jumping juniper!" he exclaimed. "I'll be a monkey's uncle! No, make that a unicorn's uncle." He put down the binoculars, shoved his truck into gear, and pulled away in a hurry. He hurried through the rest of his mail route, then went straight home.

Meanwhile, Julie and Kim had put Whisper back in her stall, unaware of what had happened. Kim stayed for lunch, then Aunt Martha "volunteered" them to help her make pies for the Greenmont Bazaar and Baked Goods Sale.

Later that afternoon Mr. Tuttle returned to the farm by a back road. He parked his car in the bushes, put his instant camera in his pocket and walked down an old dirt lane between the farms. The dirt lane ended not far from where Whisper was hidden.

Tuttle crept behind a hedge and peeked through the leaves. He saw Julie and Kim picking apples in the tiny orchard near the house. As he watched and waited, his legs started to hurt from crouching down. He rubbed them, keeping his eyes on the girls, the house, and the barn.

After about ten minutes, Tuttle saw Aunt Martha come to the back door. He heard her call to the girls. "That looks like enough apples for twenty pies. Bring in the basket now and help me peel and core them."

He waited until the girls were inside and he was sure they were hard at work on the apples. Tuttle stood up and dashed to the barn. He slipped around the corner toward the door. When he opened it, it creaked a little and he stopped. But no one in the house seemed to have heard him, for no one came out.

Inside the barn, Tuttle peered into every stall, groping his way down the rows. Pigs grunted at him and a cow snorted and stared back at him.

At last Tuttle found what he was looking for.

Whisper gazed innocently up at him. "Who are you?" she said.

Tuttle jumped back, looking over his shoulder to see who had spoken. Then he realized he had only heard the question in his mind.

"Who are you?" Whisper repeated.

"I d-d-don't believe it," Tuttle stammered. "A unicorn that talks—well, sort of."

He dug in his pocket, then raised his instant camera with trembling hands. The flash bulb went off as he pressed the button and frightened Whisper.

"Help! Help!" she cried, rearing up in her stall.

"Now hold still just a minute," Tuttle told her. The picture popped out of the camera and he hastily stuffed it in his pocket. "Just one more picture to be sure," he said, raising the camera again.

"Help! Help!" cried Whisper. She started to move toward Mr. Tuttle, who was trying to focus for another picture. He kept backing up as Whisper moved forward.

Inside the house Julie and Kim were cutting up apples while Aunt Martha rolled out pie dough.

"Did you hear something?" Julie asked Kim and her aunt.

Kim shook her head.

"I didn't hear anything," said Aunt Martha.

Out in the barn Whisper kept advancing on Mr. Tuttle. She was afraid, for she sensed that even if he didn't mean her physical harm, he was certainly up to no good. As long as she came toward him, he backed up.

"Now hold still!" said Tuttle impatiently. He couldn't focus while Whisper kept him on the move. "These pictures will prove to people I'm not a crazy gossip—and I can sell them to a newspaper or magazine for a bundle!"

"Let me alone!" cried Whisper.

Julie looked up again from her work in the kitchen. She felt nervous and uneasy, as if someone were calling to her for help, but she couldn't hear clearly. "I'm going to check on Whisper," she told the others and washed her hands.

Whisper had finally backed Mr. Tuttle up against the barn door. It swung open and he stepped through backwards, not seeing what was behind him. At that moment, Ralph bared his teeth and clamped onto Tuttle's right trouser leg.

"Yee-ow!" yelled Mr. Tuttle, thinking he'd been bitten. He danced around in a circle, trying to loosen Ralph's hold. Tuttle managed to shake Ralph off for a moment. Ralph barked and snarled, then promptly fastened his teeth on Mr. Tuttle's other trouser leg.

Mr. Tuttle tried to bean Ralph with his camera and gave up. Escape was now his only thought. He broke into an awkward trot, holding onto his camera and dragging Ralph along with him. As Whisper peeked around the barn door, Julie came flying out of the house, followed by Kim and her aunt, to see what was causing Ralph's commotion.

"I *knew* there was something wrong!" shouted Julie and ran to Whisper.

Mr. Tuttle had finally broken loose of Ralph, but Ralph nipped at his heels and jumped up on him. As Kim, Julie, and Aunt Martha watched, Mr. Tuttle did a wild dance, then fell flat on his face. Ralph put his front paws on Mr. Tuttle's back as if to hold him down. The girls couldn't help but laugh at the ridiculous sight of Mr. Tuttle and Ralph.

"Ralph! Ralph!" called Aunt Martha. "Let him go, boy!"

Ralph barked and stood aside, confused by Aunt Martha's command to let the intruder go. In the meantime, Mr. Tuttle got to his feet, grabbed his camera, and took off across the fields.

"Why did you have Ralph let him go?" wailed Julie.

"Because the harm's already been done," said Aunt Martha. "Mr. Tuttle saw what he came to see. Besides, maybe no one will believe him this time either," she tried to comfort Julie, though she wasn't very sure herself.

"But he had a camera!" cried Kim. "Do you suppose he took a picture of Whisper ?"

"Oh, no!" moaned Julie. "Aunt Martha, you should have let Ralph bite him and we could have taken his camera."

"But we couldn't have stopped Mr. Tuttle from talking," said Aunt Martha. "And I didn't want Ralph to hurt him either. We're just going to have to deal with this now that the cat's really out of the bag. Your dad's out making his rounds today but I think I'd better call him. That looked like an instant camera Tuttle had and I have a feeling he's going to be back soon—and he won't be alone. Is Whisper alright?"

"I think so," replied Julie, gently running her hands over Whisper's legs and back the way she'd seen her father do. "He didn't hurt you, did he, Whisper ?"

"No." Whisper blinked. "He just flashed a light on me from that black box he carried."

"So he *did* take a picture," said Kim.

"Was there only one flash, Whisper?" asked Julie.

"Yes. It scared me and I jumped."

"Good. Let's hope that photo is enough out of focus for people to wonder what Whisper really is," said Aunt Martha grimly. She hurried into the house to call Julie's father while Julie and Kim put Whisper back in her stall.

"I wonder why Mr. Tuttle came back," said Julie in a suspicious voice. "You didn't tell anyone about Whisper, did you, Kim?"

"Julie, I've been here most of the day! And why would I tell anyone about Whisper? She's our secret and I promised not to tell." Kim looked very hurt as she patted Whisper's shoulder.

But Julie was still full of anger and fear. "Well, it was your dumb idea to take Whisper out of the barn where Mr. Tuttle and the whole world could see her!" she yelled at Kim.

"I guess I'd better go home now if *that's* the way you feel. I can't be your friend if you don't trust me," said Kim, and with that, she ran out of the barn.

Julie bit her lip. She wanted to call Kim back and apologize, but she was too ashamed of what she'd done. She buried her head in Whisper's mane. I didn't really mean it," Julie said to Whisper. "I just opened my big mouth before I thought about what I was saying."

"You'll have to tell Kim you're sorry," said Whisper. "She's a good friend, you know."

Julie groaned. "Oh, Whisper. Everything's gone wrong, just when it was starting to go right. What a mess!"

"Don't worry," Whisper comforted her. "Maybe things will work out alright."

"I hope so," said Julie, hugging Whisper. "And I sure hope Dad gets here soon—before anyone else does!"

6

Sheriff Billings was still skeptical. This picture that Tuttle
had given him was very blurred and out of focus. It looked
as if the animal had moved and Tuttle had moved, too,
when he snapped the picture. The animal was so white
and the background was so dark and shadowy, that it was

difficult to tell exactly what was in the photograph. Sheriff Billings sighed and tossed it on his desk.

Outside his office he could hear Tuttle's voice raised in excitement, telling everyone in the parking lot that he had not only seen the vet's monster, he'd taken a picture of it, too. He was even claiming it was a unicorn!

It could be a trick photo. But it could just be a badly focused photo from a cheap instant camera of something very real. Besides, there had been those other reports last week about a giant white bird. With a crowd of excited townspeople gathering, it might be better to check out this business and quiet them all down, Sheriff Billings decided. It wouldn't hurt to drive out to the vet's place for a look. He stood up and walked over to the door.

By late that afternoon a procession of vehicles was headed out of town. Sheriff Billings' car led the way, its blue light flashing. "That thing ought to be locked up," insisted Tuttle, who rode beside him. "It's a menace, I tell you. Came right at me, breathing fire."

Ralph began to *woof, woof, woof* as the posse approached. Dad walked out on the front porch. Aunt Martha was sitting there in the rocker, trying not to think about what was going to happen.

"I can't let them get their hands on that unicorn," Dad said. "She's gentle as a kitten and hurt besides. If I know public officials, they'll ship her off to some laboratory."

"What are you going to do?" Aunt Martha asked.

"Oh, I don't know! If anything happens, it'll break Julie's heart. I've got to think of something. Would you please go and ask Julie to stay put in the barn?"

Aunt Martha found Julie in Whisper's stall. The unicorn was munching alfalfa. She looked quite happy.

"The sheriff's coming," Aunt Martha said. "Half the town's behind him. Your dad wants you to stay here and keep quiet."

Tears welled up in Julie's eyes. "They'll take Whisper away," she sobbed, throwing her arms around the unicorn's neck. "It isn't fair! She's mine, I found her."

"Hush, child. That animal doesn't *belong* to you. She ought to be free, same as you and me. We'll just have to trust your father. Rest assured, I'll have a thing or two to say to these nosey neighbors myself. I'll burn their ears off!"

Lights twinkled in Aunt Martha's brain. "Thank you," said Whisper. "You're a good friend. You remind me of Grandmother Bear."

Aunt Martha blushed. "Nonsense!" she snapped, but she was touched nonetheless. With that, she turned and marched back to the house.

"If only I had Lord Garth's magic ring," said Julie. "I'd fix them! Remember how Lord Garth defeats the tworgs? He changes himself into a giant red dragon. The tworgs get so scared they turn white."

Whisper munched thoughtfully. Outside, the sound of traffic grew louder. They could hear angry voices. "Turned white," Whisper thought. "Hmmmmm." She remembered Dorian saying, *"Unicorns have powerful magic. You're still young. You have no idea yet what you can do."*

A ghost of an idea crept over Whisper. She glanced at Roscoe the Shetland pony two stalls away. She and Roscoe were nearly the same size, though he was fatter. Maybe, just maybe. "What do you think, Roscoe? Are you willing?" she asked.

To Julie's amazement, the old pony nodded vigorously.

"We may not have a magic ring," Whisper said, "but sometimes my horn surprises me. Dorian warned me that my magic might not work in foreign lands. We'll see. Bring Roscoe in here with me. Then you've got to find a place where I can hide."

Julie followed Whisper's instructions. Old Roscoe limped into the stall and nuzzled the unicorn. As Julie watched, Whisper touched his nose with her golden horn. The horn began to glow. So did Roscoe's nose. In a second, his shaggy mane was glowing, too. Julie gasped. Roscoe's brown coat turned white!

Sheriff Billings frowned at his once shiny shoes. They were coated with barnyard mud. The veterinarian was being difficult, standing in front of the barn door with a rake in his hand.

"Now, sir," began the sheriff in his official tone, "we don't want any trouble. Tut says you've got some kind of weird animal in your barn. All we want is to see it."

"Tuttle's mistaken," said Dad firmly. "This isn't a sideshow. It's a veterinary clinic. My patients can't be disturbed."

"But doctor, if you've nothing to hide, why not let us in?"

"I told you. My patients need quiet."

Julie had crept to the crack in the barn door. She saw her father, rake ready for action. He reminded her of Lord Garth holding his singing sword, ready to defend Princess Delia and her precious secret.

"Want me to tackle him?" yelled someone from the crowd.

"Just try!" Dad shouted back.

Aunt Martha rushed off the back porch with a ladle in her hand. "I've had enough of this foolishness," she declared, pushing her way through the crowd. "What do you mean coming out here tramping over my yard? Do you have a search warrant, Sheriff? I thought not. Shame on you, disturbing the peace. Inciting a riot. Shame!"

"Now, ma'am," stammered Sheriff Billings. "It's a matter of public safety."

"Public safety be hanged! You're a pack of snoopers, that's all."

Just then the barn door creaked open. Julie stood there, facing the crowd. "If you want to see what Mr. Tuttle saw, come inside."

"Julie!" Dad and Aunt Martha exclaimed together.

Sheriff Billings hitched up his belt. "You folks stay here," he ordered. "I'll investigate." He followed Julie and Dad into the dimly lit barn. Removing his sunglasses, he saw a black and white cow, eight pink piglets snuggled against their mother, and in the furthest stall an old *white* Shetland pony. "Is that what scared Tut Tuttle?" he asked.

Dad, struggling to hide his astonishment, nodded. "Just old Roscoe. I tried to tell him." He shot a questioning look at Julie, who merely smiled back.

"All this trouble over a broken-down pony," growled the sheriff. "Tut Tuttle's made fools of us all. I'm mighty sorry, Doc, to have bothered you this way. I can tell you, Tut's going to get the lecture of his life."

Sheriff Billings stormed out of the barn. "A pony! Nothing but a pony! Tut Tuttle, you're a numbskull. If there was a law against being stupid, I'd throw you in jail. Now get in your cars, all of you, go home!"

Dad watched the cloud of dust settle in the lane. Julie put her arms around him. "You were a real hero," she said.

"How'd you do it? Where's Whisper?"

"She's hiding in the feed room behind some bales of hay. It was magic, Dad. You should have seen her turn Roscoe white. There really is such a thing as magic."

Dad looked sheepish. "You're right. It's funny. Just when you think you've got the world all figured out, something comes along and surprises the daylights out of you. Do you think I can borrow that book of yours, *The Red Dragons* of Whatever-you-call-it?"

"Sure, Dad," said Julie.

A week passed, then two. As old Roscoe's white coat faded slowly back to brown, Whisper's broken wing steadily healed. One evening Dad came into the barn alone. He was whistling, happy as a lark.

"Mr. MacMahon's mare had a foal," he said to Whisper. "She's a beauty. Pure white. I suggested a name—yours. I'd like to buy her for Julie. You'll be leaving soon, won't you?"

Whisper's eyes filled with sadness. "This isn't my home," she said.

"I know. You're almost healed. Unicorns seem to have amazing powers of recovery. I'll make a note of it."

"Your magic is good," said Whisper, feeling the strength in her injured wing.

Dad raised an eyebrow. "It's not magic, just medicine. It's something you learn."

"You can learn magic, too," said Whisper. "It's something you feel. I felt it in your hands when you helped me. Your love of all living creatures is the best magic there is."

"But I don't want Whisper to go! I want to keep her!" Julie cried to her father.

"Julie, you have to understand—Whisper can't stay with us." Julie's dad rose from his chair and sat down beside her on the sofa.

"But the people in town don't even believe she exists anymore. She's safe now!" protested Julie.

"I'm not talking about the people in town, Julie. Whisper is a wild animal. She needs to be free. She would only suffer penned up in the barn or fenced in on this place all the time." Julie's dad put his arm around her shoulder. "It's just like your mother. She was very sick and the doctors did everything they could to help her. But she suffered so much, Julie, it was almost a relief when she died because she was free of all that pain." Julie's dad paused. "And Whisper needs to be free, too. She loves us and she'd like to stay with us, but she'd only suffer. We have to let her go."

Julie turned her face against her father's shoulder and cried. He hugged her tight for a long while. "I love you," he said and Julie tried to smile through her tears.

"I love you, too, Dad," she said.

He cleared his throat. "I was going to surprise you later, but I may as well tell you now. I'm going to buy Mr. MacMahon's foal. Even though she's not Whisper, do you think you could take her in and give her a little of the love you have for Whisper ?"

"You mean, a horse of my own?" Julie looked up at him in surprise. She wiped her eyes and gave him a brave smile. "I know she won't be the same as Whisper, but I'll really try hard to love her, Dad. Thank you," Julie whispered and hugged him.

It had been a lonely week at school for Julie. Kim was still mad at Julie, and Julie was still too shy and ashamed to apologize.

The girls sat in separate seats on the bus and at separate tables in the cafeteria. By Friday, Julie was miserable in spite of her happiness over Whisper's safe recovery and Dad's promise of a horse of her own. Julie wanted to share her feelings with a friend.

She couldn't stand it anymore. On Friday afternoon Julie sat down beside Kim on the bus. Kim looked out the bus window and didn't say a word.

"Kim, why don't you get off the bus at my stop today?" said Julie. "I've got something I want to show you."

Kim turned her head. "Are you sure you want to show me—or do you think I'll tell?"

"Kim, I'm sorry. I was wrong. I said some really dumb things to you. Please let's make up. Then I can show you a surprise."

"Well—okay," Kim agreed after a long hesitation. "But I'll have to call my mom from your house so she'll know where I am." She smiled a little and Julie knew they could be friends again.

They talked for the rest of the bus ride, catching up on everything they'd missed that week. When they got off, they raced each other up the lane to Julie's house with Ralph at their heels. Kim phoned her mom, then they went out to the barn.

"Whisper!" called Julie as they entered the building.

Whisper trotted over to them, raising her head and lifting her wings in a joyful welcome.

"She's all better!" cried Kim, looking at Whisper's mended wing.

"Dad says she made an amazing recovery," Julie said proudly, but her face looked sad.

"What's wrong with that?" asked Kim.

"It means that Whisper will be leaving soon. Maybe tomorrow. Dad and Aunt Martha said I can't keep her. She'll be better off if she's free instead of hiding in a barn all the time. Dad said she would just suffer living that way. It's best to let her go. I thought you'd like to say goodbye to her before she left."

Kim put her arms around Whisper's neck. "Whisper, you're one of the most fantastic things that ever happened around here! I'm so glad I was one of the lucky ones who got to see you."

"It was wonderful meeting you, too, Kim," said Whisper. "And thank you for lending us the second Elin-sore book. It was even better than the first one."

"We finished reading it yesterday," Julie explained. "It's in the house—I'll give it back to you before you go home."

"Goodbye, Whisper!" Kim waved to the unicorn as they left the barn.

"Goodbye," said Whisper.

It was a bright Saturday afternoon when Julie led Whisper out of the barn. Dad and Aunt Martha walked a little behind. They'd draped a red horse blanket over their unicorn friend, just in case someone saw them. It dragged on the ground and looked a little silly where her horn pointed upwards, but Whisper agreed it was necessary. Beneath the blanket she now had two healthy wings. What more could she ask for except to be home again?

Atop the hill in an open space, Julie stripped off the blanket. It was all she could do to hold back the tears.

"I want to go with you to Rainbow Forest," she said.

"Someday, maybe, I'll take you there," answered Whisper, blinking back tears of her own. "Dorian would love to meet you." She looked down across the broad fields. In the distance she could see Greenmont. "This is a good place, Julie. There's love here, if you look for it. That's as good as anything Rainbow Forest has to offer. Goodbye, my friends. Thank you for everything."

She spread her wings and soared off into the blazing blue sky.

"Watch out for airplanes!" Dad called.

Whisper found that her wings were almost as good as new. It felt strange to be flying again after being grounded for so long.

Now, which direction, Whisper asked herself. She decided that she would try to retrace her flight and hope that it led her home to Rainbow Forest. But first she couldn't resist a little fun.

She circled back to Greenmont, this time staying clear of the clock and its loud *bong*. As she swooped low over the courthouse and above the town square, she saw that there was quite a crowd gathered for Saturday shopping. People began to point upward and talk excitedly when they caught sight of Whisper.

Whisper dipped her wings in a salute to them, then soared out of view. She headed for the countryside. Then she saw a tiny dot moving on the gray ribbon of road below her. "Just what I was looking for!" said Whisper with a smile.

She dived low until she hovered above the little mail truck, then flew alongside it so the driver could see her.

Tut Tuttle gasped and jammed on his brakes. Whisper flew around the truck several times while Tuttle leaned out the window and stared at her.

"Goodbye, Mr. Tuttle!" Whisper called playfully and before his startled eyes, disappeared into the blue sky.

Whisper flew for several days, taking care to follow the advice of Julie's father about resting whenever she felt tired. The clouds and birds were her only companions. She watched constantly for airplanes and steered clear of them.

At last Whisper sighted some familiar landmarks, the mountains and lakes that bordered on Rainbow Forest. And there it was—green and gold in the autumn sunshine.

Whisper glided downward and by the time she landed, a crowd of friends had gathered to greet her.

"Whisper! Whisper! You're back!" squeaked Jonathan and Bixby, hopping up and down.

"I'm so glad you've returned. You must tell me in detail about your trip," said Phineas.

Grandmother Bear wiped away a tear and gave Whisper an enormous hug.

Dorian was there, too. He nodded at Whisper as if to say, we will talk later.

After the excitement over Whisper's arrival had died down somewhat, and she had greeted all her old friends, Dorian took her aside.

"So, Whisper, you've returned to us safe and sound," said Dorian. "I'm glad."

"I'm glad, too, Dorian. I missed all of you. But I made new friends. I was even able to help them a little, I think. You were right. I have powers that I didn't realize I had. Still, I don't think the world is quite ready for me yet. Or maybe I'm not ready for the world as it is now," added Whisper thoughtfully. "There are some sad people and sad things out there—because of misunderstanding and a lack of love." Then Whisper smiled as she thought of Julie. "But there are many good things, too, Dorian."

"And I think, Whisper," said Dorian knowingly, "that in any world, you are one of those good things."

THE END